MAD to LIVE

a collection of (very) short fiction

by

Randall Brown

PS Books
Philadelphia, Pennsylvania

A previous edition of this book was published by Flume Press.
The following stories have previously been published:

Little Magpie and So Close in *Ink Pot*, You Want in *Taproot*, Just Like Flies in
Phantasmagoria, Soccer Dad in *Hobart*, The Lemurian in *Juked*, A Hint of the Void in
Word Riot, Facing Extinction and The Real in *Hunger Mountain*, Bats and Balls in *Right
Hand Pointing*, Good Kid in *Kaleidowhirl*, Sister in *Insolent Rudder*, Eight in *Laugh It off
Annual*, Mad to Live in *Connecticut Review*, Him in *Home Planet News*, Morton Bonsey in
3:00 AM Magazine, What-If World in *Vestal Review*, Whenever We Had Milk in *Quick
Fiction*, Early Man in *J Journal*, Martian in *Sou'wester*, Out of Love in *Euphony*.

The title "Hint of the Void" comes from Joyce Carol Oates's essay, "Is This The Promised
End?: The Tragedy of *King Lear*."

ISBN 13: 978-1-4583-4623-0

Cover Image: "Guggenheim" by Gary Koenitzer, © 2009, from the collection of Brian and
Yannette Digby used with permission.

PS Books
93 Old York Road
Ste. 1/#1-753
Jenkintown, PA 19046
www.psbookspublishing.org

MAD to LIVE

nothing is real until I share it with her,

and so it is with *Mad to Live*,

for Meg,

who gave life to the self I dreamed I could be

and whose beauty

every day

surpasses my capacity to imagine it

...mad to live, mad to talk, mad to be saved, desirous of everything at the same time, the ones who never yawn or say a commonplace thing, but burn, burn, burn...

– Jack Kerouac, *On the Road*

Contents

four: *what if*

Bonus tracks—exclusive to this edition!

WHAT IS one

Little Magpie

I find Maggie squatting on the kitchen floor beside the door to the garage. My eyes always go to her belly first, as if she has swallowed a globe. There've been two miscarriages, both early. Never have we gotten so far. Then I notice she's picking something off the floor, putting it in her mouth. Get closer. They surround her. Hundreds of them. Ants. Maggie is eating ants.

A lifetime of sitcoms has prepared me for cravings—pickles, hamburgers. Running out in the middle of the night for a pint of Haagen Daz Vanilla Swiss Almond. Strawberry Frosted Pop Tarts. But insects?

Maggie looks up. She removes the finger from her mouth. "Must be the baby," she says. Her hand follows the curve of her belly. "She wants bugs."

"Really? They sell crickets at pet stores. I could get some."

"Crickets?" She purses her lips, gazes up to the ceiling. Then nods. "Okay."

The girl at Pet World brings them to me in a clear plastic bag, twist-tied at the top. She holds them up, dozens of them, hopping against the plastic. "You'll have one happy lizard," she says.

"Yeah. That's all one can really hope for in life, isn't it? A happy lizard."

She nods, a sign that we share some deep understanding. She tells me she threw in an extra dozen, then winks.

In high school Maggie wrote a piece about the opening of fishing season and the senseless slaughter of the earthworm. In graphic detail, she captured the wriggling on the hook, the oozing entrails, the practice of cutting them in half to double the bait. Together we collected money, went to bait shops, released nightcrawlers, earthworms, grubs back to the wild of gardens.

At home, in the garage, I hold up the bag. A cricket stares back; all eyes, bugs are. Crunchy. Gooey in the middle. Like pretzel snacks with cheese in the center.

I picture the bugs skittering down her throat, at the bottom, a baby open-mouthed—a miracle baby. Dozens of times, the brown bleeding began, and we were told she was lost, only to see her on the ultrasound, hear the beat-beat of her heart. How useless and helpless I feel during these races to the hospital, as if there's nothing I can do for them.

I carry the bag of crickets upstairs, find Maggie lying among the dozen flower pillows, her face the center, the cushions as petals. I swish the bag back and forth, imagine her sitting up, tossing cricket after cricket into her mouth, as if chomping on popcorn.

But instead the crickets bring tears. "What?" I say. "Beetles? You want beetles?"

The crickets pop in my ear.

"I'm bleeding again," she says. "Heavier this time."

A blur—the car ride, Maggie holding the bag of crickets, tapping against the plastic, then opening it, taking one out. "She's still hungry."

The breakneck drive, the crickets, the hospital waiting for our arrival—it's all part of the blur, something to hide the truth from both of us, that nothing matters except the desires of Fate for our baby to live. But that's nothing to tell Maggie.

"It has to be a good sign," I tell her.

"It does, doesn't it?" Maggie answers, then opens her mouth and feeds our baby's desire.

You Want

The affair lingers in the most unlikely places, like at the strip mall Borders: "You want horror? It's on the other side of romance."

That affair. A terrible, selfish thing. All that it destroyed. For what? A need to be loved so desperate that it did not care what it erased in its fulfillment. Eight years of marriage. A son with anxiety and panic and compulsions so overwhelming that he clung to you as if only you had the certainty missing in the world, and you severed that connection. You sick, sick fuck.

You meet your wife for tea at the Four Seasons, where you got married, where she found you before the ceremony, alone in the Jefferson Room and said, "I know it's bad luck." She twirled in her Vera Wang whiteness and you knew you were lucky, knew the feeling wouldn't last because it never does—it passes into doubt, then into an annoyance that the twirling tiny figure can't fill anything, and then into something like revenge for what she cannot do for you.

You want forgiveness, you tell her. You want your life back—the life you had together. You want Eden, even though the apple's brown with your bite marks.

And she sighs. Because she wants that too. The gates, though, have shut behind the both of you. It's October and you were married in a long-ago August. The garden outside has filled with the burnt offerings of trees and the flowers that have given up, and you promised something in that garden and didn't live up to it—and now you want to say sorry and go back.

She's considering it. She's really thinking about it. She sips her green tea. Logan Square, outside, a fountain now dry, the flags of the world blowing against the strong fall breeze, an early blast from the north. Everyone in the window tilts, bent against something, like the bad guys on the old Batman shows. Pow! Zap! Thwap!

"Our son," she says. "Our poor broken son."

Imagine, you say, a life where you try to make up for this brokenness. You tell her that you know you never can, but imagine life with a husband who keeps trying, one who'd spend the rest of his life proving himself to her, an unending search for some action to recover her faith—each moment a choice between his own lack and his love for her. Tell her the world will try to break this husband with its emptiness and illusions of escape, but he'll endure, the possibility of recovering her love like that woman he followed out of the conference and up to the room as if she were offering salvation.

Imagine life in this fallen world. A world where you try to make up for things that you can't make up for.

"What are you saying exactly?" she asks you.

You say you're sorry, sorry you ruined everything. You know what you didn't know then, that this is the best offer out there.

"The best offer? You don't make it sound so nice."

"It is so nice. It's hard—I can't express it the way I want. I'm saying I get it now."

She finishes the green tea. You know she's resisting the temptation to say, "Yeah, you got it alright." Instead, she asks, "Why did you have to tell me about it?"

Because it hurt. Because emptiness is better than that awful horror of how easily you could crush things. Because that terrible selfishness that wants the end of things. "I didn't want you to find out some other way."

"How would I find out—the girl?"

"Yeah. The girl."

She rings the mug with her ring finger. "Oh. I can't do what you did to our son. If there's any chance of saving—Aw. It's just so. Nothing. So nothing nothing nothing."

You did this to her.

"I'll never. Never ever," you say.

And she believes you, because she wants to save things, important things, separate from her. Her unselfishness. Do you get that?

Months later, as you toss the football to your son so he doesn't feel worthless on the field with his friends, so he doesn't tremble in the car unable to go out and face things, you stop thinking back to that dark room and Rachel, who promised a world without those things that pulled you back, and you stop thinking of yourself as some kind of hero for returning home and making things right again. Because you look at your wife, your wife on the wooden chair with her dark glasses and her head buried in books about chestnut hair blowing in the sea breeze and endings where even dead people get together and find each other, your wife who never looks up to see her son running toward the ball rather than away from it and her husband throwing each successive pass with a little more zip into his open chest.

So Close

It was Lucy who agreed to swap with this couple from Iowa they met on the airplane. He wondered how it came up, but didn't ask. They seemed nice enough to him.

Maybe it's what we need, Matt, Lucy told him. She faltered over the "we." She had recently dyed her hair red, as if that would be enough.

Whatever, he told her. If you think it will help.

They all started in the same bed, but Lucy got up with Ned and went onto the couch in the suite's living room. Dottie, Ned's wife, told him she was ready as soon as he was. A pale lumpy pillow. That was Dottie.

His hands. Wasn't sure what to do with them, what was off-limits. So he held them behind his back, heard the couch in the living room thump against the wall. It sounded like "Love Me Do," the way wiper blades swish to the radio.

Dottie said she wanted to switch; he rolled over.

Our son, Edward, she said. He's one point away from a genius. You got any kids?

He shook his head. I guess I should tell you, he said. I don't have orgasms. So whenever you're ready.

She whistled. Like a machine, she said. Not ever?

No. I get close, though.

And that doesn't drive you nutty?

He had accepted this fate, this life without orgasms. But not Lucy. It filled her with guilt. He was ahead of her in the giving department by hundreds of them. There was no catching up.

It still feels good, he told Dottie.

Dottie moaned, and he wanted to put his hand over her mouth, wanted to say that they were right next door, they might hear you. Wanted it to matter.

Dottie's face red now. He imagined a swirling ball of matter, like the Big Bang, twisted in his stomach, suspended there, unable to explode. A machine, Dottie had said. Mechanized, yes. Kept it from becoming something intimate, so much so that Lucy was with Ned, and he only felt relief. Finally. Someone else's turn.

Yeah, Dottie said. That's good. Keep doing that.

Of course, he could. Forever, as long as it took. He thought of Lucy's contorted face, her sinking into the couch, Ned with her. My God, she might say. I forgot. That's how it's supposed to work.

And then a shriek from the living room. Again. Lucy. He pulled away.

Dottie pulled him in. I'm so close. Please.

He felt pulled elsewhere, grabbed a robe, ran in, found Lucy on the couch, face red, Ned on the chair, eating M&M's from the servi-bar.

It broke, Matt. He looked at the shred of latex on the coffee table. You know what that means?

He stared at it, the white globs, the force and violence of this explosion. His mind had the conception of it —Ned's sperm in a mad dash, leading to what? Baby, adoption. Would Ned be involved in the decision? Dottie? Maybe they would all live together, Ned screwing Lucy and Dottie, and he'd change diapers and fill bottles. Odds were there'd be no baby, maybe just some disease Ned would give them, something incurable but not deadly.

Well, did you? Lucy asked.

No, he said.

Close?

He shook his head. Lucy shook hers.

Well, I was close, Dottie said. Real close.

He and Lucy laughed. It felt good to laugh with her. Dottie and Ned looked horrified. And that added to the uncontrollability of it all. They laughed forever after about that blown-up rubber, Ned's frozen terror, and Dottie, angry, because she had been close, real close.

Cadge

They borrow things from her—not just dye-free Tide, the organic jumbo brown eggs, a cupful of lactose-free milk. They borrow her brown Coach bag, her Barbara Heinrich pearl-gold bracelet, her Donald Pliner shoes, her Jane Bohan ring, her black Prada dress, her Infiniti G35, her pool for birthday parties, her house for the meet-and-greet for parents of new students. They borrow her wireless Internet access, two feet of the south property line, the occasional Sunday paper. At one time, they borrowed her social security number, her Platinum American Express, her CAP account.

They borrow her husband. They fly him to Cleveland, Dallas, Palm Springs, Atlanta, Boston. They borrow him for dinner, for Saturday meetings, for Sunday golf with clients flying in from Japan, India, California, skiing in Tahoe with the attorneys from Frisco. They borrow his easygoing charm, that fierce determination for that thing beyond the thing he has.

Take them, she tells them. I don't want them back. She takes longer and longer walks, farther and farther from home. She imagines the notes posted on her front door.

There must be more, one of the notes will say. And a note from her husband.

Long ago, he knocked on her apartment door, she answered with

"What do you want?"—and found him and his wrinkled bow tie. "Twenty-seven times," he said. She stood behind him, on tiptoes, with no idea how to tie it, but the first try—voila! Wrapped like a present. At the wedding, it began. Her father said, "I need to borrow him for a moment." How far that moment has stretched, continues to expand.

Her husband's note could say *Missed you!* But it won't. I'm missing something, it'll tell her. She'll come home to find out what's gone, the something her husband can no longer name.

Just Like Flies

I catch her in bed with Spiderman, in the late afternoon and after sex, the bedroom tossed about as if at sea, and I'm yelling at Spidey to show himself, unmask, I'm telling her to stay out of it, but Spidey maintains the calm of the super and heroic.

Mask? he says. What mask?

There's always a mask, you freak, you wife-fucking, web-walloping freak.

She's still screaming—something about costumes and make-up—and I want to kill someone but I don't know who.

The three of us, her legs over her side of the bed, Spidey dangling over my side. Me at the foot of the bed, breathing hard. The one window letting in the slanted day, like the tilt of a camera and the obliqueness of comic book pages.

First your mask, Spidey says. Then we'll talk.

Now, he's in charge. That's the way it is with these guys. I want to know why, a why that stretches long past masks and webs and beds and the three of us. I want to know what love is like above the world, if it subsides like here on earth. I think of a long ago feeling we might have shared, then didn't and couldn't recapture, and there's the question.

Did you find it? I ask her.

You don't have to tell him, Spidey says, like I'm the bad guy who needs to be hung upside down until the cops come. That's how it is, huh?

Okay, I say. Okay. I give up.

I reach my hands back around my neck, search for the edge or a fold, but it's imperceptible if it's there. I try my nails, try digging—and feel the tiniest border between me and mask. Oh this is how it begins, the ripping of a face into a half, the twisting of a mouth into something wicked and half-right. I'm on the precipice—and she doesn't scream, but leans forward, exhales sharply. Spidey poises himself to fling his unbreakable webs.

The skin tears too easily, and I sense Spidey about to spring. I *am* the bad guy now. I'm the one leaping out the window, the one caught between here and there.

Spidey's on my tail. Her head's out the window, screaming something I can't hear but sounds like *sorry* or *hurry*—and then I'm out of skin and self, strangely light, particle, wave, a free thing, faster than the web-slinger's threads that would tie me to earth. The shredded self finds her in the window. She waves it like a banner, and I shouldn't have looked back because earth is rising to meet me, the dirt of it, the hard crust.

Here it comes—the all of it.

Whenever We Had Milk

My father would pick up the milk glass and pass it before my eyes. "Past-your-eyes" milk, he'd say. Every time. One can't help but wonder about such things, about what awful thing he thought would happen if, just once, he'd forgotten this ritual.

In the milk box, I once found his lover's dress. Another mystery. Who had put it there? It smelled like old cheese.

I kept it under my mattress, and one day when I came home from school, my mother sat on my bed, the dress on her lap.

"Yours?" she said.

"A girl," I said. "From school."

"Fifteen year old girls don't wear this." She held it up. It took form, filled with her body, this lover. She had red hair and meat, lots of meat. She was made of steak. She bled and that made me think of that week in fifth grade I'd asked my mom about periods and she said it's when you begin to bleed down there and I waited until I finally figured it out, that it belonged to the girls. I'd get dreams, wet ones, and it was nothing like that.

"She's older," I told her. "She doesn't care that I'm fat. She likes me for me."

"Yeah. That's a load of crap." She tossed the dress at me and it brushed against my face.

My father came home. I heard them yell upstairs. I sat at the table with the glass of milk. I picked it up myself, passed it in front of my eyes, said that incantation aloud.

two

WHAT FOR

Soccer Dad

My son sucks at soccer. Look at him—playing with the string on his shorts, chewing his lip, watching the ball roll by. Pathetic. The coach looks back at me, sitting in my lawn chair, PowerBook on my lap. As if it were my fault. As if I am one of those fathers.

Alex runs over. Water break. This is your mother's fault, I want to tell him. She's the one who twists her ankles when she tries to run, hits the badminton shuttlecock backwards, dribbles the basketball off her feet. Blame her.

Instead I ask him if he's having fun. Water dribbles down his chin. Yeah, he says. I kicked the ball to Connor. Wasn't that cool? I reach down, tie his shoelaces; maybe I should tie them together, bind him to the lawn chair.

Yeah, yeah. If he doesn't care, why should I? He can't help it that he sucks. But I also can't help it that I care. Grant me that, at least.

The coach talks to Ben's dad, Jeremy's dad. Slaps them on the back. They laugh. Your kid, he sure can play. Whatever you're doing, it's working.

I estimate that, out of twelve kids, Alex is the third worst. Jack actually sits down on the field and Hayden spends the entire game celebrating some imaginary goal. Their fathers are lucky; the kids suck so bad that clearly it must be some wiring gone wrong. Nothing could be done there.

Full of signs, the world—and they flash here like the oranges, reds of the players streaking toward the ball.

You, the signs all scream. *You suck at being a father.* No wonder I'm trying to hide.

I peek above the screen—just in time to see Alex looking over at me and the ball speeding to the side of his face. He crumbles like a cookie. Crumbs of Alex lie on the field.

I rush out. Alex kicks at the ground, holds his face, and cries, of course, loud wounded sobs that echo from field to field so the other games next to us stop.

Suck it up. Walk it off. My own father's voice, I hear. I played an entire baseball game with a broken wrist, a football game with a separated shoulder.

On his face, a red splotch spreads, like something spilled. I pick him up, think of the way Boo Radley picked up Jem and carried him home. Alex stifles his sobs against my chest.

We sit on the ground along the sideline. Sniffles now. An occasional tremor through his tiny frame.

And then Alex says the magic words, the words I've been waiting to hear, the release from this hell: Dad, I think I'm done with soccer now.

I will carry him to the car, wave good-bye, get him a Happy Meal, take the top off the convertible, hold our arms up as we fly away.

But parenthood is about pain. That's what my father taught me. So I suck it up.

Your team needs you, dude, I tell him.

Really?

I rub his face, hold him. He stands up with a few minutes left. Coach pats him on the butt, sends him out.

Alex waves to me as the ball rolls by.

The Lemurian

My new neighbor Jack says he's half-Lemurian, this ten-year-old boy with no father, freshly re-planted here in the Philly suburbs, dreaming up a spiritual connection. He wonders how his father will find him here. I get it, after I Google "Lemuria," part of Mt. Shasta mythology, an alien race from a lost continent of a lost age of bridged continents and rising waters.

"They are an advanced race," I tell him. He nods. He stands in his yard; I, in mine. He wonders about my kids, my wife. In one scenario, I imagine telling him the truth—how I blew it, how I fucked this graduate teacher, how I confessed and wasn't forgiven and sacrificed the kids we might have had and ended up here, talking to Jack, looking at his wide wet deep brown eyes and thinking and then rejecting the idea that he has some power to recover for me all I've lost.

Instead, I tell him I never had these things.

Today, Jack holds a Chargers' Nerf football. He sails it as if it were the fathership coming for him.

"But," Jack says, "they can't leave the mountain. It used to be an ocean, you know. All of it. I bet my father can breathe underwater."

"How 'bout we toss the ball," I say. "You there. Me here."

Jack's roundness—chipmunk cheeks—and his long eyelashes are evidence enough for me of his advanced lineage. He throws me the ball, end over end. So maybe evolution doesn't involve throwing spirals. My return throw bounces off his hand, deflects off his head.

Of course I imagined him leaping into the air, catching it one-handed, somersaulting backwards and bouncing up to his feet—*ta da*—forgetting how I dreamed as a kid of things I didn't have. Like a home I wasn't ashamed of, that didn't need to be kept hidden like a pile of shit in my pants.

A couple more throws, the ball careening off every part of Jack's body. Each time, he calls out "Oh God" and chases the ball here, there, everywhere. Then, with a bang of the screen door, his mom appears, calls Jack to the house and replaces him on their side of the yard. She's so desperately thin that I can see why the Lemurians might be irresistibly attracted to her bones and her translucent skin. Her name is Madeline, like Roderick Usher's sister, buried and resurrected.

"What do you want with my son?" Her voice, full of grit, as if coming from a deep chasm.

Jack tumbles back toward her, Sisyphus's rock, her rock, up and down, across the country they rolled. Jack got beat up on playgrounds. Jack drew Lemurians as family portraits. Jack's desperate desires won't be assuaged. Jack rolls down the hill.

"He reminds me…" But I don't know what to say after that.

"He's just Jack." He lands beside her. She rubs his ear. "He's nothing of yours."

"Hey, Just Jack," I say. "And what do you want with me?"

He lifts up his shirt, points to his back. Madeline scratches. Jack closes his eyes. "You aren't my father," Jack says.

"No one believes us," Madeline says. Her eyes the green of Rolling Rock bottles. Her black hair blows into her face, creating the illusion of a veil.

"I want to believe you," I say. "And Jack, if anyone comes and says he's your dad, well, you better make sure he can fly or have gills or some kind of proof. And me…" I could lift up my shirt, show them the red scars of childhood burning there still, only the wind sweeps across them, blowing them back up the hill, mother clinging to son.

"I've got nothing, Jack. Nothing."

A Hint of the Void

Helen left. One moment brushing the dog, searching for kids' snow pants on the Internet, a load of laundry, repeating spelling words, making Livy write "odor" three times, instead of "oder," arguing with Spenser about the need for a shower. Sometime later, a blink and then her absence. The note said simply, "I am not Mother."

An hour into her absence, Spenser said, "I'm sick." "Me too," said Livy. Theo rolled on his back and whined softly. Seth felt it too, empty-headed, with deep aches and a stomach that rose into his throat. They sat in the family room, around the unlit fireplace. They huddled together. A winter storm beat against the windows and roofs. Trees bent in their attempt to loosen and crash against the house. A voice threatened them, taunted them to come outside. They drew closer.

"I think we're having an existential crisis," Seth said.

"If you say so," Spenser said.

"That sounds stupid," Livy said. Theo yawned wide and long.

"Life is like Halloween. No one makes their own costumes," Seth said to the kids and dog.

"Maria did," Livy announced. "She was a toilet. You pushed her lever and she said 'swoosh.'"

"You mean if you took away all the rules?" Spenser said. He reached for Theo's chew ball and threw it against the wall. "I'm playing ball in the house."

"Stop it!" Livy yelled. "Mommy hates that."

Seth sometimes wanted to grab Spenser and plaster him against the wall. He sometimes wanted to buy him everything he wanted. He wanted to eat a thousand doughnuts with Livy. He wanted to throw ice-cold water in her face when she ignored him. He wanted to watch television with them all day. He wanted to leave them and be a fly fishing guide. Leave for a year and write his novel. He wanted to let them all sleep in the same bed. Spike their orange juice with Xanax. The world—with its Gravity and Momentum and Time and a million other unseen forces—held the dark, deeper desires in check.

Helen did the same for the family. Kept them from Chaos. The storm crackled and blew and split the world into inside and out. Helen was out.

Spenser threw the ball against the wall, again and again. Livy screamed nothing but a scream. Theo buried his head in his paws.

The door flung open, the cold and wind rushing toward them—and it was Helen. She held milk, cocoa, and marshmallows.

"Mommy!" they all screamed and buried her in their relief.

"It's hell out there," she said.

The door blew shut.

Facing Extinction

One night, Isaac comes to my bedroom with his forehead full of wrinkles and his lower lip almost touching the floor. "Daddy, Daddy, a meteor killed all the dinosaurs…"

The red tail of the meteor burns in Isaac's eyes, forever falling, covering the world in dust.

"Did you have a bad dream?" I yawn and prop my head on the bedside table with my elbow.

"No. The show said that…the TV."

I try to shake off the sleep fog.

"Daddy…that show."

"Okay. Okay."

"I was thinking of the dinosaur babies. What happened to them?"

"The babies?"

"The babies in the eggs. Did they die?"

Isaac's lip begins to tremble, his legs too. The eggs, the babies, that's what flashed in his eyes. Cracked. Shattered. Millions of dinosaur eggs. What does he picture inside each one? A tiny mouth open, a little scream?

"A terrible thing," I say. "What happened to them."

Maybe it was his anaphylactic allergy to eggs. In Zany Brainy last week, his grandmother handed him a plastic egg and he threw it back at

29

her. His legs shook and he didn't know why.

"Daddy?"

He reaches for my hand, wanting something else, some certainty, some answer that has nothing to do with these eggs he can't eat. And I know what my son wants, what I wish I could give him: Heaven.

My mother didn't allow us to believe in God, or an afterlife. "Remember, those things are for people not in their right minds," she'd say. She negated that world, but never told us what to believe instead. A world full of meteors that could crash down at any moment, without purpose or meaning.

"They lost the world," Isaac says, sniffling now. I reach for a tissue; he cups it in his hand, sets it on his nose, leaves it there. He doesn't blow, afraid his brains will burst out.

"You and I," I say. "We came from their world. Out of all that dust."

"So?" he says. He crawls into the bed, sits on me. "You aren't a dinosaur."

"No. Not yet."

He laughs a little and falls on top of me. All I know to do is hug him tightly, feel his collapse, his body weighing against mine, his tremors slowly subsiding. And soon he is asleep, still on top, twitching a bit, dreaming perhaps of his father and everyone he knows hatching from the dust. But I feel an eternal wakefulness, as if I'll never fall into that deep sleep again, not because of meteors, flames, apocalypses, but my son, of course. How little and how much of him rises and falls, how, beyond any imaginings, the world will break his heart.

Early Man

My son finds the envelope, outside the stadium, bloated, like when our Bichon ate an entire challah. He counts it in the car. Everyone's leaving but us. Two-thousand dollars.

"I think we should keep it," he says. "I mean—anyone could say it's theirs."

He's fanning the money like he's holding a poker hand. Well, too many cards for poker, but it's like that. On the envelope, someone has scribbled, "For Emergencies." I ask my son what our emergency might be.

"I don't know," he says. "Finding this. Figuring out what to do." Officers walk by, looking for drunks staggering to their cars. "I guess we could give it to one of them." He points to a policeman. "But, I mean, it's Philadelphia. They'll just pocket it."

"Well, maybe they deserve it. More than we do. They do get killed a lot in this city."

I've turned the car and the radio on. They're talking about the game. It ended badly, the Eagles stopped at the goal line, predictably, an entire history of such moments.

"We could put it back," he says. "It's making me—I don't know—nervous or something."

I've already pulled into traffic, already inching toward the expressway, an early exit, near Penn. How did that happen?

"I bet college students could really use it," I say.

He's counting the money again. "If only we could know how it was being used. I mean for a real emergency. I know what mom would—would have—said."

"Yeah. We both know what."

I'm stopped again, between Penn and Drexel. She'd have said, "Keep it. Go somewhere."

"Let's go," my son says. He has a wide smile, fanned out, like all those bills.

We're outside Madison Square Garden, looking for Police tickets.

"I used to do this for the Dead," I say. "Way back when."

My son finds a guy. He wants $500 a ticket.

"Dude," my son tells him, "the concert's about to start." My son pulls me over. "For the old man?"

The guy walks away. My son tells me to wait, and he's right, the guy comes back and it's $500 for the pair.

We sit in the lower level, to the side of the stage, about ten rows up. My son points out the old guys doing their dances out of time.

"This is great, Dad," he yells above Sting's de do do do.

I notice some of the younger girls check him out. I stay in my seat, not wanting to embarrass him. I wonder about the money, imagine it belonging to a ticket scalper, and that makes me feel better. I had a summer of the Police a long time ago, *Synchronicity*, Sting walking among candles on MTV.

We order room service dessert, coffee and cookies and cupcakes. We stay up all-night watching movies—*Stand By Me, Signs, Spiderman, Jaws.* My son falls asleep at sunrise, and there's still something left to do, I'm sure of it. My son mumbles in his sleep. My ears feel unpopped, ringing from the concert. It feels like I'm on a plane, going somewhere, maybe to Lake Como with my wife. We ran into Elton John at a market. For the rest of the honeymoon, I couldn't get "Rocket Man" out of my head.

Later, we're in an evolution store in Soho looking at real dinosaur eggs and woolly mammoth hair.

"Something totally useless," my son repeats. "That would be perfect." He's pointing at collections of penis bones—coyote, fox, mink, raccoon. The bone itself is called a baculum. He choses a skeleton of early man, a "Lucy" replica.

"Early man was named Lucy?" I say on the way out.

"It's better than baculum" is his reply.

He sleeps on the way home, and I have to stick my head out the window to stay awake. The skeleton lies in the back seat. Sometime near the Pennsylvania border, my son says, "I'm glad we did this, Dad. I mean—it felt different. Really different."

Sometime later, a siren. I wonder what the police will make of the skeleton in the back, and feel that rush of fear as their car gets closer, then whooshes past.

"Not us," my son says. He turns around to Lucy in the backseat. "It's okay," he tells her. "No need to get rattled."

He winks at me, thirteen, on the verge of things. He holds up what's left of our cash, opens the window, there it goes.

three

WHAT NOT

Bats and Balls

I let a fly ball sail over my head, hit off the top of the fence, bounce over for a homer. If I'd have dropped it, my father might've showed some understanding. But my standing there, "still as a statue," that was beyond his ability to comprehend. I was thirteen.

We won anyway, but Dad wouldn't let me go to Dairy Queen. Instead he went to the Falcon and returned with the bat and basket of balls he kept in his trunk.

When I thought I loved him, I ran over the entire earth to catch his monster launches, hurdled over the shrubs at the property line, ducked under the tetherball, ran straight through crabapples that smacked against me.

Maybe his passion for physics explained his love of the fly ball and my intuitive gift to be under the ball no matter its trajectory. He took his AP students to baseball diamonds and pool halls. He'd smash drive after drive until he could whack them level, so that he could prove a dropped ball would reach the ground simultaneously with the hit one.

Baseball. My father's love. They were entangled, like the webbing of a mitt.

My father stood at home plate and said I couldn't leave until I shagged a hundred fly balls. But I was done with baseball. The first fly ball sailed over my head. I sat down, cross-legged. After a dozen, my father started to aim for me, long looping fly balls that thudded yards, sometimes feet away.

Dusk. Pink clouds. The type of light balls got lost in. Soon line drives whizzed left and right and over me. It was as if a shadow swatted the balls over third base, curved them toward me in left field.

I found my father's collection of *Playgirl* magazines in his closet. They weren't there when Mom lived with us. Bats looked like giant boners— and I pictured my father holding the bats of the men in magazines and heard the playground names for him, felt a deep fear, as if he had a sickness we had to keep secret.

I wish he had found me that night with his wild line drives, picked me up and carried me home.

Good Kid

In walk these two hombres through the swinging doors of the pool hall. They're both skinny, hands grease-black, uneven beards. As they pass the tables, each grabs a cue. Corey's beating the crap out of THE DOMINATOR, a whole hour on one pinball. He's twelve years old, mouth burning from Wise barbeque chips and the Mr. Pibb chaser.

His grandfather plays the part of the hero who rides into town and saves him. Each summer and every holiday Pap takes Corey up the mountains and into the nowhere town of Huntingdon, with its boarded-up shops and silent streets. Corey sometimes runs the snack bar and register, sweeps the place, loads the Coke and snack machines, and takes out the quarters. Pap has long silver hair in a ponytail, leather hands like an old baseball mitt, the power to read thoughts, eyes with the force to push you back against a wall.

That's why the breath leaves Corey when his grandfather collapses under the first blow from the cue stick. The stick breaks across his forehead, down he goes, like nothing. Blood leaks from the cut. Corey makes a squeaking noise. The pinball drops down the hole and THE DOMINATOR laughs and says in his menacing voice I WILL DESTROY YOU.

"Kid. That your pappy?"

Corey nods.

"He'll be okay. Just knocked out. You keep a secret, all right. Wouldn't want to have to visit you some night."

One of them's punching at the register, but nothing's happening.

"You know how to get this open?"

Corey shakes his head. The one at the register pushes his grandfather onto his back with the cue stick. He holds the cue over the slash in his grandfather's forehead. Corey knows this scene, from the hundreds of Westerns Pap and he watch together. His grandfather's the thing that will make Corey do what they want.

The other guy, he unzips his pants, pulls out his thing. "Maybe I'd like to get this sucked, too. That wouldn't be so bad, would it?"

Corey coughs up chewed-up chips and the fizz of soda and some breakfast eggs too. He reads books he shouldn't read, Stephen King, about a guy in prison who tells this gang he'll bite it right off if they put it in his mouth. Corey's dad left because he couldn't keep his hands off his son.

"Not that," Corey says. "I'm not doing that."

The cue stick gets rubbed across the gash in his Pap's head. Corey had to bleed from his butt before his mother believed him. Now she can't look at her son. Now she stays away. Now when she sees him, she sees the man hunched over him too.

An ax hangs next to the fire extinguisher, by the side door, between Corey and the men with their cue sticks. What if he could chop them up? He might end up in some crazy house, with dreams of cut-off arms and legs coming for him. And if he did what they wanted? What then? There's his Pap's shotgun, too, but Corey doesn't know where.

"Get the fuck over here."

Corey does. He walks past the ax.

"That's a good kid."

Corey stands in front of the man with his purple thing that looks like a swelled-up bruise and its pumped-up head he keeps shaking. Pap groans. What if he wakes up and finds Corey with this thing in his mouth? His grandfather will become like Corey's mother, unable to look at him without seeing this man and his thing too. "Good kid," his father called him, for saying nothing, doing nothing.

Corey kicks the guy's balls hard, kicks them like he kicks THE DOMINATOR'S ass day after day, kicks them so fast and hard that his foot is a flash and even when the guy's dropped to the floor, Corey doesn't stop.

But it isn't over. The other guy jumps up on the counter and down in front of Corey. His mouth, twisted into a snarl—yellow teeth that match yellow eyes, yellow greasy hair. A wild thing, escaped from a cage.

Corey clenches himself into a dead thing, a thing that cannot feel, cannot be hurt. The cue raised over him, ready to crack, get inside, break those things Corey makes unbreakable. But the stick never lands. Instead the pool hall explodes and there's a hole in the guy's chest.

Pap holds the shotgun. They both stand still, taking stock of each other.

"The world's full of 'em," Pap says.

Corey still can't move. There's that jagged hole. The puddle of blood. The insides prepared for a blow that never comes. A father who whispers in his ear, "You make a sound, any sound, and you're dead."

Pap. He stands tall and defiant. The one thing Corey cannot live without. He won't leave his grandfather. He will be deputized. He will have a posse and walk the silent streets by his grandfather's side. He won't go back. All this spills out to Pap, mixes with the hard ringing in his ears, the smoke and awful smell of sweat and burnt blood.

The grandfather doesn't hesitate. He grabs Corey and pulls him into the dusk. A siren cries out, draws near. And when the dreams of the men with their bloody holes haunt Corey, he fights them off with this moment, the pink sky, the leathery hands, the two good guys and their walk into the far-off sunset.

Sister

At the end of *Gatsby*, Nick imagines the first Dutch sailors arriving at the "fresh, green breast of the new world." Earlier, the car that killed Myrtle Wilson tore off her left breast.

The encyclopedia lists slang terms for women: *birds, hens, chicks.* The encyclopedia warns that these might be slightly offensive. Feminists, the encyclopedia says, use sister.

My sister's breast cancer. Her risk factor—reaching thirty-six years old and having no children. And her mother's breast cancer. And her mother's mother's breast cancer.

God grant me the serenity to accept the things I cannot change, / Courage to change the things I can, / And the wisdom to know the difference. This prayer can also be found in *Slaughterhouse-Five*—on a plaque in Billy Pilgrim's office and in a locket between the breasts of his caged, naked Eve on Tralfamadore.

In any definition, dictionaries mention "two" and "milk." Normally two. Milk-secreting. The source of affection, emotion, and nourishment. Or something that looks like one of the two milk-secreting organs— such as the breast of a hill.

Hers is aggressive, wants her to die, her cells to stop growing, differentiating, repairing themselves. After our mother died, I told her she should consider a mastectomy. She would, after she had her children. She used the word "suckle." I giggled and she punched my arm and I mouthed words to her during the funeral service. *Nipple. Suckle. Booby-Trapped. Children.*

At the end of *Cuckoo's Nest*, when McMurphy attacks Nurse Ratched, he first rips her uniform away to expose her "big womanly breasts." Then he tries to strangle her, forever silencing the Nurse's mouth, described earlier as "a doll's lips ready for a fake nipple."

Dwight Wesley Miller, a Texas art gallery owner, exhibited a mural of the creation of bare-breasted Eve. He was told he would be prosecuted because he was exposing children to hardcore pornography. So, he covered the breasts with yellow tape that read "Crime Scene."

I never met the men, only heard about the endings. Scott in college said he could never marry a white woman. Aaron in law school told her only if she lived in New York City. Terry took her to the mountains and said he had the spirit of lone eagles. Alex already did the kid thing. Sam demanded that she be debt-free first. How uncertain they left her, how hollow. I've learned what men want, she told me. Not me. I laughed, thinking she was joking.

Aurorae Australis. Bazooms. Cupcakes. Dutch Alps. Explosives. Feed bags. Grab-Ems. Himalayas. Isaac Newtons. Juggernauts. Kumquats. Love Pillows. Mommy Bags. Nuclear Warheads. Oppenheimers. Praise Gods. Queen Missiles. Rockies. Sierra Madres. TNT's. U-Boats. Volcanoes. World Trade Centers. X-Rateds. Yahoos. ZZ Tops.

From an advertisement for fake breasts: *Men and women agree. They both prefer bigger boobs. Adam & Eve, a company for sex tools, has done research among its consumers about what the perfect breast looks like. C-cup was preferred by 42*

percent of the men and 45 percent of the women; B-cup, the first choice of only 24
percent of the women and 14 percent of the men.

I was ten, my sister fourteen. The door ajar. They were untouched by light, a whiteness of hidden, secret things. In the mirror, she touched them, all around them. And then I got it—she was searching for lumps. All her life she searched for them.

Later, after the mastectomy, after the prognosis of blood vessels penetrated and the cancer cells lodged elsewhere, in the spine, the lymph nodes, I sit with my sister.

It wasn't about the children, she says. I didn't think anyone would want me without them.

I Google everything I can about breasts. Do you think a bull, one site asks, is interested in the cow's udder before desiring her? What does the bull think of instead? Of the flutter of her eyelashes, the splash of spots across her side, her lolling tongue? I search and search and still don't understand what I am looking for.

We hold hands.

I've never touched a breast, I tell her. I can think only of poison instead of milk.

You could've sucked the poison out. (Ha.) You've touched other things, yes?

Yes.

She puts my hand on her indented chest, and I don't know what then. I lie there in the bosom of my sister. I feel the vigorous beat of her chest and all that it has hoped for and waited for and will never receive.

It's okay now to rub her chest, to bury myself in it, to kiss her scars.

Eight

My mother tied my arms to the bedposts so I couldn't touch each eye eight times, squeeze the end of all eight fingers, circle my lips with my thumb eight times, find eight curls to twist. Before the rope, some nights I got that far; other nights, I didn't even finish the eyes before she grabbed my wrists, but she could only hold on for so long. The rope made me hold on tighter to my world. I allowed her the illusion of victory. I counted and touched myself in my mind and convinced myself her sickness could not touch me. How much pride she took in her cure, in the terrifying decision she made to encircle my wrists with twine. For love. To save me. Eventually—a month, a year, I can't remember—she unbound me and I deluded myself that I was free.

Figure eight as double four. Figure four as half of eight. If you skate, you would be great. If you could make a figure eight. That's a circle that turns 'round upon itself.

Thirty years later. *Remember all those eights*, she says, as if they disappeared. *Those crazy eights. Like a needle in the deep scratch of a record.* Eight worldly dharmas—the traps we fall into: to want praise, a pat on the back; to avoid criticism; to want success; to avoid losing; to want happiness; to avoid sadness; to want acclaim; to avoid anonymity. Suffering ends when desire ends—thus the ropes.

My mind has little room for anything else. It isn't cluttered like most minds—just absorbed. *You never thanked me*, she says. *It wasn't easy. Believe me.* Thank you, I say. Does she realize there are eight letters in *thank you*—that I'm wearing eight pieces of clothing: two socks, underwear, pants, THE DOORS T-shirt, button-down collared over-shirt, DA EAGLES hat, PHILLIES wristband.

She never stops. Her courage. Her act of love. Her terror. Her decisiveness. Her worry. Her being driven crazy. Her cure. Her redemption. Nothing ever ends, ever settles, in this world. And I'm so sick and tired of forever.

Hold me, love me, hold me, love me…

Eight stabs, stopped by bone, missing the heart. They'll add them up and tell her "eight." I always counted—she never knew how much.

Mad to Live

They stripped my father's bed, separated his clothes from his verses. For a while, he scratched Lowell's poems into his own tablet—the black and white composition notebooks of grammar school. The mattress has blood, urine stains. I wanted to be here with—no that's a lie—so I came too late.

Pan, of shepherd and flocks, appeared to Frost on "naked pasture land." It's the sudden anxiety of loneliness that inspires Pan—who tore Echo to pieces and flung her over the world. I've read hundreds of my father's critical articles—his tearing into Frost, Lowell, Bishop, Sexton, Whitman, Eliot. Like Hawking looking for the Theory of Everything, he desperately wanted to discover the one sentence that, once uncovered, would reveal the mind of the gods. No one gets that in this world. Certainly not someone immersed in so much verse.

He hit me last visit, months and months ago. "Where are you? Where are you?" He didn't believe me when I said, "I'm here." He struck me with his fist. "You never understood." At twenty-two, I had handed my father my first poetry chapbook. He had wept, held my head in his hands that felt like worn catcher's mitts. "You'll try," he had said. "How hard you'll try." Later, whenever I visited him at his prep school hidden among Maine evergreens, he always looked wrung out, like a man who didn't know how to breathe. I showed him some recent work, maybe the condom spread I'd done, the man and woman fallen in daffodils, the caption *Trojans...for the love of your life.* "A lot of people see this?" he asked. I nodded. "Your name?" he said. "I don't see it here." He turned the page upside down, looked on the other side. "I don't see it anywhere."

The gods' punishment for my father? They curled his fingers so he couldn't write; they blackened sight so he couldn't read. They undressed his words, exposed him to nothingness before he was ready.

I open my father's notebook. It begins with a quote from Lowell, who for a time had tried to live without poetry: "I was naked without my line-ends."

I sit in his classroom, spare as a cell. Nothing remains. I listen for the echo of my father's voice, wanting to hear my name, but only a whisper of Frost, more questions, what to make of a diminished thing?

"Oh God!"

I jump at the voice.

"I thought—oh God. You're Seth. Dr. Levitger's son. I'm Diane. Next door." So young. In a painting in my father's den, Echo's curves contrasted the sculptured hardness of Pan's human torso; demure, her gaze avoided his desire.

Up, I walk around the blackboards, the dust smell still in the air. "I can't believe you know who I am. What did he say? When he mentioned me?"

"Oh. Well, he'd show us your advertisements. He once asked me, 'Where am I here?' But, well you know, he was like that. Always looking for himself in everything."

"And what did you say? I mean, how did you answer him?"

"You had that one image of the homeless woman caught among thick snowflakes." Yes. Soap flakes, really. The actress like all the women I pursued, barely there, as if that was all I was worthy of. "Her request—change—had that multitude of meaning your father liked. And the images have that archetypal feel. I told your father he was there. He didn't buy it, though. He didn't think it mattered much."

I stand over his desk. Everything looks small. My father was a colossus. "Because I was selling stuff."

"It lacked eternity."

"And my father's sales pitch?"

"I don't know, Seth. He grappled with the cosmos—not condoms."

Diane's voice rings with vibrancy, authenticity. My own sounds tinny and small. She's slight as a reed, but she bellows her words. At my father's desk, the wooden chair is hard and cold, the desktop empty except for a pile of note cards. "What are these?"

"He passed them to the students. The will of the gods. And when students enacted Oedipus or Antigone, the ones in the audience were supposed to boo or cheer the actors' actions based on what their cards said."

I flip through them, written in that clear, strong stroke, so unlike the shaky lines of his final notebook. *Mortals must fear death. Mortals must be brave. Mortals must obey their kings. Mortals must remain loyal to family. Mortals shouldn't think they know what the gods want.* I begin to sense the irony of my father's position, drenched in uncertainty, yet convinced of the rightness of his beliefs. He thought he knew, but he was just guessing. And what if he guessed wrong?

"You're a disciple," I say.

"I guess so. He had such passion."

"Not for people though," I say. She loved him. As a daughter to a father? Or something else? My mother left, never to return. My father hated the flesh, loved the uncorporeality of pages that couldn't love him back. Diane's flesh and vigor excite me the way line breaks thrilled my father. An odd desire, the urge to swallow her, fill myself.

Truly, in such a world, it's my father who doesn't matter. I see him atop a rock tower, eyes on heaven, his body bowed.

Diane probably doesn't see my father this way. I imagine her love remained of no substance to my father, and I wonder what love might she have for me, this lesser version of him, one not meant for the heavens but the earth.

"We should go to dinner," I say.

"Why would I do that?"

"I don't know," I say. "Maybe it's okay to believe in the world. To sell condoms, change, vacuum cleaners, shampoo, deodorant." I finger my father's cards. *Mortals must fight the boundaries that confine them.*

"Okay for you," she says, an echo of my father. She rubs the wood of the doorframe tenderly. And I could tear into her, anatomize her, rip apart her heart and still find nothing for myself.

Martian

On the outside of the envelope I sent to a girl in Mars, Pennsylvania, I wrote, "Check for hidden bomb. This means you." I'd danced with her at my cousin's Bat Mitzvah but had nothing to say afterwards. I pedaled to the Hampden Township pool, sat alone on my towel reading another book about far-off worlds, while somewhere across the Susquehanna River, what I wrote, like someone yelling fire in that crowded theater, evacuated a building, sent sirens from East Shore to West Shore.

My name crackled into the space above the pool summoning me to the office. There two guys dressed like the agents in *Close Encounters* waited with questions meant to make me crumble, and once I saw the shred of envelope, I confessed. They wanted remorse, so I gave them tears and sorrys and the shakes, but after they left, I rode home in a rush, a Willie Stargell card in the spokes like the beat of a song, and I knew what I wanted: to capture its notes, send them off, wait for the call of sirens, crying out, "Here I am. Here I am. I am here."

four

WHAT IF

The Real

What if no one died?—and no one touched you?—and no one drank anything but Ginger Ale and no one smoked even a candy cigarette and no one beat you with straps? What do you get to explain yourself? Imagine wishing for those things—the drunk mother, the perverted uncle, the militaristic dad. That's the sickness I got—the desire for the story that provides the edge to define me.

Here's what I mean. As our sorbets—now turned to soup—are being carted off, I ask Sally to tell me something about herself.

"My parents were nudists. I grew up with nude naked people. Everywhere I looked. There they were."

Dang. I got covered-up parents and vacations at the Jersey shore. Sucks.

"Like Eden," I say.

"Yeah, just like that. Except for two towels, one to sit on, one to dry off with."

"I can't wait to see the family photos," I tell Sally. She has orange hair, like Annie. I keep waiting for her to break into song. But she doesn't. Maybe tomorrow.

"Family photos? That's getting ahead of things," she says. "What about you? What did you have?"

I lie. I'm used to it. I'm a writer. I've made up hundreds of childhoods. "It's weird, because my mother was like an anti-nudist. A germaphobe. We had to be covered up, no skin showing ever. And the showers. Six of them a day. We had thin, red skin. Our veins shone through."

"Opposites attract," she says. "Think if we met as kids. You trying to clothe me, me trying to undress you."

Yeah. Just like that. We go home, undress, shower, and Sally can't believe the perfection of it, not only its length but its girth. And she's seen lots of them. She tells me, though, she can't touch it. Not ever. They sicken her, the bigger the sicker she gets. Something left over from nudist camps and blob-like men who should never ever be seen unclothed.

I can touch her, though, she tells me. All I want. Wherever I want.

Of course there is no Sally, no penis of perfect length and girth, no dessert, no nudist camps, no towels, no blob-like men.

What is there, really? Isn't it strange that you, reading this, are the only reality, the one real thing in the entire transaction from writer to text to you. And all you get are lies, strung-out sentences chasing the Real that always eludes the period.

What did you do to get such a world? What happened to you? What has made you Reader and me Writer?

Opposites attract.

You so real, the only truth to be found in this world, faraway, like naked Sally running along a beach that isn't Eden, because Sally is so full of desires—to be blinded, carried away, invisible, born into a family with clothes. And she is the embodiment of something, something Real that, once understood, means something entirely else, some connection that explains what has allowed Reader and Writer to meet here, and not somewhere different, that has to do with covering and uncovering, touching and untouching. You and me and all that the world has promised but never delivered.

And what of Sally, left naked on a towel, aware now of Writer's selfishness and self-regard? She's dressed, driven away and remembering her childhood, those awful folded bodies that have come to define her.

Him

It begins at Whole Foods, with sideways looks and secret gestures, murmurs following me down aisles, building as I read the labels: natural, organic, no msg, zero trans fat. I ask the cashier if she notices it, and she nods her head. I ask her if she knows me—no; if she knows what I've done—not a clue. I can't wait to get home, search for myself on the computer, but I can't find myself there, only a family tree an uncle planted in some virtual nowhere. Nothing in the local news—the national, international, entertainment, sports, science. Nothing. Nothing. Nothing. It must be the computer.

At the Apple store in Suburban Square it starts up again. They're getting bolder. Pointing outright now. "It's you," the Apple girl says.

"I didn't do it," I tell her. "I didn't do anything."

I get the sense it's more ridiculous than horrible, what I've done, the bad kind of fame, but the kind that goes away, like colds. I'll wait it out. I've got the groceries and the will. I'll root it out; if anyone knows the secret of search engines, it is I. I've found diseases my doctors have never heard of, secret words that unlock the cheats and prizes of software, women twisted into impossible places. When I find it, I'll post a picture on lampposts and store windows and telephone poles and I'll write in black permanent strokes "I'm not him," and then they'll know. Everyone will know.

Morton Bonsey

A computerized random name generator gave Morton Bonsey his name. I wonder what Morton wants; most of my characters want to inhabit discarded bodies—that of my grandfather, aunt, mother, brother, ex-es—but Morton feels different. He wants his own body and life. I'm not sure how to give him that.

I put Morton in a diner because I've never been in a diner. It's silver and has a jukebox at each table. It's called Wolfie's. They specialize in Boston Cream Pie. Morton drinks the half-and-half containers. Morton wants his own desires and I'm lactose intolerant. He orders the pie with ice cream. He orders milkshakes. He gets tiny containers of Lucky Charms and puts half-and-half on them.

He's stretched out thin, though. He wears Oakley sunglasses. He has sun-bronzed hair. He does dangerous things like dive off cliffs and surf tsunami-size waves. He smiles sincerely at the too-heavy waitress. He likes her. He could take her home and know what to do. He could love her.

He flicks through the jukebox offerings. He likes unironic songs about America and picks a Garth Brooks one. The waitress likes him too. It's the end of her shift and she'll go with him. Morton wants to come to my house. I wait for him and the waitress—Corrine—

downstairs by the unlit fireplace and the vacant television. I leave the door ajar.

"I want something different," Morton says when he arrives and sits on the couch next to Corrine who weighs almost as much as I do. He's a bit wound-up.

Corrine is placid, just there. I'm not sure why she's there. She has a beehive hairdo and doodles on her order pad. She draws pictures of poodles.

"Whatever you want," I tell Morton. I say this because I'd like Morton to be happy, for someone to be happy—and why not Morton?

"What should we ask for, Corrine?" When did they become a "we"?

Corrine looks up, continues to doodle. "I'm not sure what a man like that can get for us, Morty." Morty? He's a Morty now? "Maybe we could just stay the night."

They do. Their lovemaking hammers through the house like contractors working on a renovation. Then footsteps and Morton knocks on my door and walks in. He sits on the blanket chest at the foot of the bed.

"Your happiness," he says. "It worries me." He waits but I don't have anything to say about it. "Corrine's a real knockout. Thanks."

"I had nothing to do with it, Morty."

"If you say so."

In the morning, Morton's gone. Corrine's all broken up. She fixes lactose-free pancakes and we talk about Morty, what a great guy. "Nothing like you," Corrine says.

"I know," I say. "That's what I liked best about him."

"Me too," she says. She goes on a crying jag for a while. I wonder what Morty would do. He'd be a rock for Corrine. I let her lean against me. She smells like suntan lotion and oceans and faraway paradises where Morton Bonsey rides waves and sunsets and worries about my happiness, of all things. We are alike, Morton and I, after all. We both want to live.

Out of Love

Lucy believes—the way she trusts gravity, getting old, being lonely—that she does not matter in this world. If she could talk to me, writing her, she could not form the words to ask for help, because she does not grasp the lie at the center of her Self. I want so much to save Lucy, but I don't know how.

I whisper the terrible truth into her dreams, that in some ways she is right to think she doesn't matter, because her mother's drinking has not a single thing to do with Lucy. The same thing would happen no matter what daughter she pushed into her world.

"Lucy, you matter." But that voice, Lucy knows, is a lie.

There must be something. Some action. Maybe a boy. A boy with a guitar, verses in his pocket, a thousand verses, all about Lucy, not just her thousands of freckles and her green, lit-up eyes, as wide as golf course greens. But about Lucy's heart. How full of holes her heart is. How he loves the fact that Lucy cannot eat when she is away from home. How her shyness hides a strength, a will to go on, to want more from the world than it can offer her now.

But then Lucy will learn that she matters only when boys love her. It will lead her to an alley with her math teacher, a desperateness in her grip of his shoulder, the pull of him greater than gravity. He will turn aside from her lips. Is he heroic or chicken for changing his orbit? Sick. He must be, but I don't know him. I only know the black hole it will create inside Lucy.

I'm so sorry, Lucy, I wish there was another way. But you will suffer alone a long time. You will find solace in books, desire transformed to journey.

I love you. I wish that mattered for something.

In college, you are the girl around which they gay men circle Something both safe and hard about your desire for them. They understand invisibility. They love your pink, oval glasses, your wild scarves. They love your laugh, call it a titter. Tittering Lucy. You sometimes take ecstasy, sleep in a pile of men, all wanting something other than you, but it's okay. The ache of longing is better than the nothingness of before. You will stay in Chicago after graduation. You will work in customer service at a newspaper. The entire city will call you whenever they are missing sections or receiving nothing. You are a smile. A promise that is sometimes broken. You memorize the script until you forgot that part, think the words are your own creation. Eight years will pass like that, Lucy.

And then, when you least expect it, you will hear a whisper. It will say go to 815 West Oakdale. Someone there is missing something. Deliver it. Ride your purple bike. Wear your pink hat and your pink glasses. Knock on that door.

Your mother chose drink over you, a million times before, a million times after. It has nothing to do with you, Lucy. You matter.

Will you go? Will you listen? I wish I knew, but I don't.

Maybe you do know. Maybe you find me, still writing this story, trying to matter. You peek over my shoulder, point to the screen.

"That's me," you say. You rest your hand on my shoulder. You smell like the world before everything falls. "Call it 'Out of Love.' That's how you wrote it. I can tell."

The ending nears, one too ho-hum and clichéd for readers.

"They're just jealous," you say.

Jealous of us. As if we mattered. Imagine that, Lucy, if you can.

What-If World

I alight upon the branch in the willow tree with the secret knot-hole full of crystals, stream-smoothed rocks, dried daffodil petals.

"There you are," Annie Rydell says. How strange to see the elfin features—the milk-white face, the thin layer of freckles, the tiny nose and ears, the wild red hair—that appear in the women in my stories, story after story. Annie as the porn store clerk, the subway R.E.M. fan, the wife behind the surgical mask, the agoraphobe confronting the white birch woods.

We are ten years old. In the next moment my mother will reach up and grab Annie's leg as she descends from our willow, will catch her—or more accurately, get in the way of Annie's tumble through the branches. My mother will pick her up, shake Annie as if she isn't real, and spit into her face, "I'm tired of your mother fucking my husband."

The white streak of my mother's hair will burn. Her face will curl up into a fist that she will hurl at Annie. Annie might fall backwards from the blow, except my mother will hold her in her too-tight grasp.

I will fall, too. I will unhook my mother's fingers from Annie and push my mother away from her and to the ground. My mother's head will bounce off a root. She won't wake up right away.

I will reach for Annie's arms, imprinted with my mother's claws, only Annie will twist away from me, run past the ten houses on Meadow

Lane to her own house. I will climb back up to the branch and gaze down with my bird's eye upon my fluttering mother under the umbrella of the weeping willows.

But that is the next instant. Now Annie and I sit, our hands interlaced. Her breath smells of Swedish Fish, her lips glittering with pixie stix dust.

"I could never unlove you," she says. The crystals in the secret knot-hole, only the ones she sprinkles with the dust and breathes upon seven times, protect me at night, allow me to sleep in spite of the fact that someone could bury me alive or the house could catch on fire or murderers could come with swords and firebrands.

"But what if you didn't live here?" I ask. "What if you were born in France or Australia?"

"What if? What if? Why do you live in *what-if* world?"

"I don't. I'm just saying."

Sometimes there's silence and I cannot even hear her breathe.

"The stars," she says. "Let's wait for them. I think they're just there."

"Just there? Why?"

"So we can wait for them."

"Oh." I didn't understand completely, not then.

Maybe I tell Annie then how she is my best friend. How I cannot sleep without her breath upon the crystals, cannot talk without halting when she's away. Maybe I tell Annie Rydell there is the willow tree and her—and all the rest is unlove.

Maybe we just lean against each other, baby cheek to baby cheek, waiting for the stars, and maybe this time the door never opens and my mother never strides toward the willow tree and I don't un-alight from the branch and disappear back into what-if world, far away from Annie Rydell, just there like the stars, to give the world its wonder.

About the Author

Randall Brown directs and teaches at Rosemont College's MFA in Creative Writing Program. He appears in *The Rose Metal Press Field Guide to Writing Flash Fiction: Tips from Editors, Teachers, and Writers in the Field* and in *The Norton Anthology of Hint Fiction*. His work has been published and anthologized widely. He is the founder of Matter Press, its online magazine *The Journal of Compressed Creative Arts*, and the blog FlashFiction.Net, whose singular mission is "to prepare writers, readers, editors, and fans for the imminent rise to power of that machine of compression, that hugest of things in the tiniest of spaces—micro, sudden, flash, fiction." He lives in the Philadelphia suburbs with his wife Meg (co-founder of Mutt Match, a non-profit organization bringing shelter dogs and families together), their two kids, and a lovely pack of pups. He also enjoys fly fishing, the outdoors version of this world of (very) tiny things.